Isaac Ferris

Address Delivered at the Opening of the Law Department of the University of the City of New York

SALZWASSER
VERLAG

Isaac Ferris

Address Delivered at the Opening of the Law Department of the University of the City of New York

Reprint of the original, first published in 1859.

1st Edition 2022 | ISBN: 978-3-37513-104-3

Verlag (Publisher): Salzwasser Verlag GmbH, Zeilweg 44, 60439 Frankfurt, Deutschland
Vertretungsberechtigt (Authorized to represent): E. Roepke, Zeilweg 44, 60439 Frankfurt, Deutschland
Druck (Print): Books on Demand GmbH, In de Tarpen 42, 22848 Norderstedt, Deutschland

ADDRESS

DELIVERED AT THE OPENING

OF THE

LAW DEPARTMENT

OF THE

University of the City of New York,

ON THE 25TH OCTOBER, 1858.

BY

ISAAC FERRIS, D.D., LL.D.,

CHANCELLOR OF THE UNIVERSITY.

PUBLISHED BY
THE COUNCIL OF THE UNIVERSITY.

1858.

Members of the Council.

Gardner Spring, D.D.,
Hon. Myndert Van Schaick,

Mancius S. Hutton, D.D.,
James Brown, Esq.,
Robert L. Kennedy, Esq.,
Francis Hall, Esq.,
Hon. A. W. Bradford, LL.D.,

Thomas De Witt, D.D.,
George Griswold, Jr., Esq.,
Henry Van Schaick, Esq.,
Hon. Wm. B. Maclay,
John T. Johnston, Esq.,
James Suydam, Esq.,
Isaac Ferris, D.D., LL.D.,
Thomas C. Chardavoyne, Esq.,

Wm. Curtis Noyes, LL.D.,
John J. Cisco, Esq.,
Waldron B. Post, Esq.,
Wm. W. Chester, Esq.,
George Potts, D.D.,
Thos. Suffern, Esq.,
John C. Green, Esq.,
George W. Bethune, D.D.,

Leonard W. Kip, Esq.,
Wm. W. Phillips, D.D.,
Thos. H. Skinner, D.D.,
Adam Norrie, Esq.,
Charles Butler, Esq.,
Paul Spofford, Esq.,
Wm. M. Vermilye, Esq.,
O. Bushnell, Esq.

Officers of the Council.

JOHN C. GREEN, . . . President.
JOHN T. JOHNSTON, . . . Vice-President.
HENRY VAN SCHAICK, . . Secretary.
WM. M. VERMILYE, ... Treasurer.
ISAAC FERRIS, D.D., - . . Chancellor.

Members Ex-Officio.

His Honor the Mayor.
Wm. Tucker, ... Alderman.
James Davis, ... "
S. A. Bunce, ... Councilman.
Jas. M. Cross, ... "

At a meeting of the Council of the University of the City of New York, held at the Council Chamber, November 11, 1858, the following resolution was unanimously adopted:

"RESOLVED, That the Address delivered by the Chancellor, at the opening exercises of the Law Faculty, be printed for distribution, and that the subject be referred with power to Committee consisting of the President, Messrs. Johnston and Vermilye."

Extract from the minutes.

H. VAN SCHAICK,

Secretary.

The following Address was, by arrangement with the Law Faculty, purposely restricted to general University topics, leaving to His Honor, Judge Clerke, the Senior Law Professor, the whole field of remark on the importance of a proper mode of law education; a subject which he fully discussed in his calm, judicious and able manner.

The publication of the Address was deemed desirable by the Council, in order to meet the inquiry, "What has been accomplished?" made by those who had contributed to the establishment of the University, as well as to show to our fellow citizens the precise ground the institution occupies, and its advantages for education.

GENTLEMEN OF THE COUNCIL OF THE UNIVERSITY:

GENTLEMEN OF THE RESPECTIVE FACULTIES:

GENTLEMEN OF THE ALUMNI:

RESPECTED PATRONS AND FRIENDS:

I congratulate you on this auspicious occasion. Every stage in the onward course of an important object involving the interests of society mentally, morally, or physically, furnishes ground for congratulation, and especially is it so with the attainment of that high point where cherished plans are realized, and the results show that labor and liberality have been well employed. This is our favored position to-night.

It is now some twenty-nine years since the first serious consultations concerning the establishment of a New York University, and at that time plans and various details were submitted to a chosen few, in the study of a venerated minister of this city, who has gone to his rest, by the Rev. Dr. Alexander Gunn.

The sudden decease of this excellent and able

man laid aside for the time all action on the whole subject. Frequent conversations, however, in the circle of those who had been before convened, led to renewed conferences and with an enlarged circle, including some of the most intelligent and distinguished gentlemen in the various professions, and in mercantile life, in this community. There seemed to be a remarkable coincidence of views on the importance of a University movement. It was in December, 1829, that the first record of their consultations was begun, and it indicates that devotion to the great work, that patience and punctuality in frequent meetings, those enlarged, liberal and practical aims which one always expects in such men, and which call out our admiration. Alas! the larger proportion of those eminent men has passed away—yet a goodly number remain in the mellowness of age to rejoice in this day.

They early threw out before the country the great outlines of their plan.

The eclectic feature had a marked prominence in their minds; while the more usual course as regards science and letters—i. e., requiring a full course of classical studies as well as the mathematical and Belles Lettres for the Baccalaureate of Arts—was provided for, they saw the necessity of giving a distinct place to the preferences of those who might not desire the classical curriculum, or did not deem it necessary, and this was one of the special features of their plan. But they looked beyond the academic, and embraced in their range of aims to be accomplished, the professional as well—what a noble and comprehensive plan theirs! It embraced:

1. A Faculty of Lettres.
2. A Faculty of Science and Arts.
3. A Faculty of Medicine.
4. A Faculty of Law.

Being composed of representatives of different religious denominations, or in other words contemplating a union institution, they could not add the Theological Faculty.

The enterprise on which they entered was one of comprehensiveness and magnitude.

To build a great institution is a work of labor and of time. Years must necessarily be occupied, and happy they who, after the exercise of great patience and liberality, see their undertaking rising on a firm basis, and standing in good working condition. In the history of nearly all our best institutions it is found that their early stages were attended with difficulties and discouragements, which, only after years of anxiety, at length yielded to faith and perseverance.

Much has been said in recent years about "full-orbed universities," and about a great Central American University, or a Metropolitan University. The theories are beautiful, well defined, and of amplest range; we subscribe to them heartily, and believe in due time they may to a large degree be realized. But were vast funds donated, and professorships created, something more is needed for effective and successful operation. We cannot force the public mind. Men will not come to your halls merely because professorships have been instituted.

The principle is as sound in education as in economics, that the demand must precede the supply. There are, it is true, some modifications to be made in special cases, but this is the rule. The want leads to the requisite provisions, and only when a people are prepared for it—i. e., have a sense of the want—can success in any movement in that direction be expected. The early stages of a people are controlled by *the practical*. The higher state of sufficiency, when plans of personal aggrandisement have been extensively realized, and masses are relieved from the pressure of the merely practical, will bring the period of the æsthetic and all that relates to ornamentation and artistic gratification—in a word of that which, though it belong to science and art, may not be convertible to practical ends; and then will come the expansion into the higher regions of thought and investigation, when the cultivation of distinct departments will find ready devotees, and a general interest in the same may be awakened among the mass of society.

On these principles it is, that only in old countries, which have grown rich, or where numbers are found not controlled by the ruling aim of pecuniary accumulation, that the verification of the theories of full-orbed universities occurs. In our own country the day will no doubt come, when they will be found here, attracting large numbers, perhaps thousands, to their halls. Until that period the practical will predominate, and what is not apparently convertible to the purposes of life, will not command success. The American University must in this view be built up gradually. The leadings of a felt-want on the part of the public must be followed, and provision be made to meet it. And in due season they who come after us, will see in beautiful expansion and in as beautiful harmony all the departments of a complete educational system. In the meantime let theories prevail, and men rush on to vast projections, which by half a century precede actual wants, and the result will be what it has often been, the expenditure of much money and a harvest of chagrin.

Some of the originators of this university, I have no doubt, had views concerning its immediate and great expansion, which the history of no similar undertaking warranted, and in some cases, perhaps, thought that they might, by a leap as it were, reach magnificent results. But could they be present on this occasion, I cannot but believe they would rejoice in the fair and abundant results of all the patience, and all the perseverance, and all the liberality exercised.

It will be my aim, my respected auditors, to hold up to your view the actual system now successfully prosecuted under our charter, to show you the practical character of each advance in our expansion, and how the public wants in our range of duty are met.

This will lead me into some detail, but I am persuaded you will bear with me, as it is fitting to this occasion, and as we may well desire to give our friends the resumé of our first quarter century.

Our system has three distinct stages:

1. 𝕿𝖍𝖊 𝕻𝖗𝖊𝖕𝖆𝖗𝖆𝖙𝖔𝖗𝖞.
2. 𝕿𝖍𝖊 𝕮𝖔𝖑𝖑𝖊𝖌𝖎𝖆𝖙𝖊.
3. 𝕿𝖍𝖊 𝕻𝖗𝖔𝖋𝖊𝖘𝖘𝖎𝖔𝖓𝖆𝖑.

1. 𝕿𝖍𝖊 𝕻𝖗𝖊𝖕𝖆𝖗𝖆𝖙𝖔𝖗𝖞.

This is, it is true, not a part of a university course technically viewed, yet it must be acknowledged as bearing the same relation to it as the portico to the building, or it may be said more strongly, as the foundation to the edifice.

In this the young mind is led through the elements of various knowledge usually acquired in the grammar school, and here as the youth advances he may be fitted for higher scholastic training, or for the counting room or commercial life immediately. So important do we deem this to be, that its careful oversight and stated visitation are parts of the duties of the Faculty of Science and Letters.

2. 𝕿𝖍𝖊 𝕮𝖔𝖑𝖑𝖊𝖌𝖎𝖆𝖙𝖊.

In our *Collegiate course*, which constitutes our second stage, we cover precisely the same ground as other colleges, aiming to give the highest possible tone to the instruction imparted, and to inspire youth with love for literature and learning.

But we stand here on the *eclectic ground* of our founders. While we might individually prefer that young men should take the full course, and would so advise them, yet they or their parents have ever selected the parts of the course to be pursued. A decided proportion of our students has always been of this .description, taking the Scientific and Belles Lettres studies, or one or the other, having in view what may be most available in subsequent pursuits.

And what have been the results? In the course of our *first twenty-six* years there have graduated as Bachelors of Arts 536 young men, while some 400 others have to a larger or smaller extent enjoyed the benefits of our instructions. This will compare favorably with other institutions of a similar character. By an examination of various catalogues we find that in the first sixty-six years of Harvard the graduates amounted to 531, in the first forty-five years of Yale to 524, in the first fifty-one years of Columbia to 541, in the first thirty-two years of Princeton to 506, in the first thirty years of Bowdoin to 541, in the first thirty years of Dartmouth to 644. Our venerable and venerated compeer in this metropolitan field, Columbia College, was seventy-five years old when this institution was opened, and in the twenty-six years in which we have labored side by side we have graduated about the same number.

Now, to those results of a literary character it may

be added, that while our graduates in Science and
Letters are found in various mercantile and professional positions, accomplishing all which their
young alma mater, now in her twenty-sixth year,
could have anticipated, and are filling also professorships in several institutions of learning, about one
in *three* and a small fraction have devoted themselves
to the ministry of reconciliation, and are doing a
faithful service in the pulpit at home, and on the
vast missionary field abroad.   These are results which
we commit to the consideration of the friends who
have aided our cause in time of difficulty and doubt,
as showing that their kindness has borne its proper
fruit.

I ask you to pass with me now to a notice of our

3. Professional Departments.

These constitute our *third stage*.   We are all àware
how the great solicitude of parents is directed to the
future of their sons rapidly passing to maturity, and
that the practical tendencies of our country converge
on that point.   Thus from 17 years of age, (if not
earlier,) what I call *technically*, the professional want
predominates, and even abbreviates in many cases
the general literary course.

This has been met.   We have first our

School of Art,

sustained by one far from being unknown in the

department to which he has devoted his talents and taste, and who gathers around him every winter groups of those whose tastes and proposed pursuits for life lead them to the cultivation of the æsthetic art—Thomas S. Cummings, of the National Academy.

In the amazing advance of internal improvements in our country, there has grown up a demand for men especially educated to take charge of, and carry through, the enterprises which the purposes of business call into being. The profession of the *Civil Engineer* has accordingly a distinct, honorable, and most important place, and takes rank with others. To meet this want, we have, secondly, our

School of Engineering,

in charge of one who to his mathematical attainments adds familiar acquaintance with the whole field over which he conducts his classes, and whose young men are abroad in the world ably sustaining the honor of the department—Richard H. Bull, A.M.

It is now sixteen years since the third—the

School of Medicine,

was opened. What it is, is well known over our whole land, as its graduates are found in all parts of our country, and who occupy its professorships, and dispense instruction, my fellow citizens know particularly—they need no endorsement of mine. The graduates last year were 127, and since the opening of the school have amounted to 1847.

Allied to this very closely, is the demand for education for the preparation of the medicaments so largely used in our country. Hence 4th, we have our

School of Practical Chemistry,

a most important and ever indispensable complement to the physician. Such a school not only places the druggist on high and independent ground; it embraces in its range of studies the principles of chemical research, as applied more particularly to agriculture and the manufacturing arts; in a word to an extent it performs the work of a school of mines.

Now in these, departments unitedly, during the last year, there were enrolled 573.

Thus by the processes *now pursued* in this University, we may say to this practical age, give us your sons at ten years of age, and with due diligence on their part and co-operation on the part of parents, we will, under a favoring Providence, return them to you, on reaching their majority, well trained in science and letters, professionally qualified as *artists, engineers, physicians, chemists,* and from this time we shall be able to add, as *lawyers:* nor will our work stop here; governed by the same practical principle, we shall still follow the law of demand, whatever it may be, and adapt ourselves to it. Indeed, the indications are that we shall be called early to other expansions. By the organizations already in operation, there are forty men now engaged on this course of instruction.

On this summary review allow me to make two

or three remarks: 1. This work has been accomplished without *municipal aid.* There have been no city grants to sustain us, no appropriations annually even in our greatest straits, though we have been doing a large gratuitous work, and beautified the city by one of its most noble edifices. Nor have we been favored with any special state grants beyond the marble, for our front. The Legislative appropriations which were received during several years were not in the way of endowment, but to aid principally in current expenses. Our work has been one of stern effort and of great self-denial.

2. All this success has been won in the face of a fearful weight of *pecuniary pressure.* It is well said, that it is no credit to one's discernment, after a work is done, to see how it might have been improved. So it may be said to myself, when I remark, with all deference to the first laborers, that it was impolitic to undertake to erect a great institution, with a provision of means only sufficient to put on its first tier of beams.

The necessary consequence of entering on this work with only a subscription of $100,000 was the creation of a debt, and that constantly on the increase. In the midst of the work, or rather when quite incomplete, came the business prostration of 1837, which will be long quoted for its severity, and which brought from the window of not a few palatial residences the red flag of the auctioneer. It was a time that filled most minds with consternation; alas! what it must have been in cases of the heavy pressure of indebtedness, whether churches or institutions of learning. In our case it was fearful.

Immediately preceding the entrance of my predecessor, Mr. Frelinghuysen, on his duties as Chancellor, in 1839, (I am unable to speak of the amount previously expended,) there was a permanent debt of $90,000, and a floating debt of $70,000. The latter was paid by friends preparatory to his coming. The next report of the Finance Committee gives an indebtedness of $100,000, and annual expenses exceeding income by $2,400. In 1845 it was reduced to $73,900, and was (with list of some $25,000 conditional subscriptions) about the sum of debt when the 2d Chancellor removed to his present station. The final payment of the entire indebtedness was made in June, 1854.

It is not a question for discussion now whether anything was wrong here, and what, if anything. The creation of the first indebtedness will explain all that followed, to those who know how rapidly such a burden increases when societies begin with debt, and are committed to a specific policy. All we have to do with this matter now is, to note how like a mountain weight it tended to press down the University for over twenty years. It would seem to be sufficient to crush out its life. But notwithstanding such a weight on her bosom, the University lived and went on with her work, and was sending out her noble bands of young men to the arena of life.

The catalogue of oppressive circumstances is not complete until we note the unhappy divisions which arose among her corps of laborers. Several times were there serious conflicts previous to 1839, the merits of which this is not the time or place, nor would I desire to speak. They are only referred to historically, to remark how necessarily painful and disastrous in their influence on the public mind they must have been. It cannot tend to build up an institution, to have her instructors and officers arrayed against each other in the public print, (a house divided against itself,) and had there not been an essential vitality in the University, the result would have been fatal.

The question may be asked, How was all the indebtedness removed? It is a fair question, and I am happy to answer it. It has been liquidated mainly by the large liberality of mercantile men in this community, or of those whose wealth was originally accumulated in commercial pursuits. I am proud to say, that in this institution, this superb edifice, you look on a memorial of the noble liberality of large-hearted merchants. We are their institution emphatically.

It is proper to say, that since 1854 we have had no indebtedness beyond current bills, which the current income meets. Under the stern, necessary rule adopted by the Council in 1850, that no debt should be incurred beyond the yearly receipts, our way has been relieved altogether of the preceding anxiety. It is true, that unless the institution be flourishing, or has adequate endowment, independent of patronage, the effect of this economic course comes heavily on the corps of teachers, reducing their compensation, if there be a deficiency or loss—a result of painful character, and to be regretted. Of the wisdom of this position of the Council there will be but one opinion among practical men; and it will evince clearly what ground for confidence the community may justly have in the men who have carried this institution through such crises; indeed, it invites their benefactions in order to secure more enlarged usefulness.

A third remark I submit is this—in the progress of our course this institution has contributed, through its professors, to the great interests of science and society, by various issues from the press, and marked honor has been accorded to their contributions.

These productions are known over our whole land—they are in our best institutions—they are everywhere quoted with the highest respect, and as authority. Several of them take place with the productions of the most distinguished men in Europe.

Some of the successful efforts of our professors have ministered, and are ministering largely to human comfort, and the higher civil and commercial interests of men, and have secured pre-eminent honor to the University.

How amazing, how world-wide, how delightful the art of painting the human face by the power of light, whether it be called the Daguerreotype, the Photograph, the Ambrotype, or the Kalotype. It was but a few yards from the spot which we now occupy that the first successful experiment was made, and the art thrown out at once to the world, that all might enjoy the benefit of a discovery so happy— by our *Draper*.

And there are some here to-night who witnessed the first public exhibition of the electric telegraph, in a lower story in this building, which Prof. Morse, of this University, had conceived, and had been for several years here perfecting. Let us judge of the importance of these discoveries, by conceiving what would be the condition of society if we could now, in an instant, be deprived of Draper's Daguerreotype and Morse's Telegraph.

Our work, I repeat, is by no means done; as fast as the public want shall indicate the demand, expansion in other directions will occur, and other schools or departments will be organized.

One is to be inaugurated to-night—our

Law School

or fifth Professional Department. This was contemplated in the first consultations concerning the University. The conviction was deep and unanimous that rare advantages are afforded by our city for both medical and law schools; and these advantages have decidedly increased since that day, and point most clearly to New York as *the* place where the intended medical practitioner or the lawyer can be, above any other part of our country, qualified for his responsible position.

An early movement was made towards establishing a Law School by the appointment of some of the most eminent men at the Bar, but it was soon seen that the want was not so felt as to encourage the continuance of their efforts. Since that time the demand for a well-arranged system of legal instruction has been widely felt and earnestly expressed. We have been pressed from various quarters for several years to the action which has taken place, and every effort has been made to secure the right men to meet the public desire. Public announcement has been made of the honorable gentlemen constituting the Law Faculty, and unanimous approbation has been conveyed to us by personal communications and by the press. Their work from this day they begin. The accommodations provided for the exercises of the school are ample and commodious, and I invite you to inspect them. The field of instruction by Lectures will be comprehensive of all which the wants of the profession require, and to this will be added such practical exercises as will bring into application what is communicated by the lectures. It will be to us a matter of peculiar gratification, if, by this complement to the Faculties contemplated by the founders of the University, we may confer extensive and lasting benefits on the community in which we live, and on our common country. By this evening's action we shall stand as a completed whole.

We naturally look with pleasing anticipations to final success in accomplishing all in the detail as well as in the general, which a Wainright, a Cone, a Milner, a Broadhead, a Crary, a Thompson, a Gallatin, a Delafield, a Lewis, a Johnston, and others of our early, but now departed active co-operators proposed. Our progress will be slower than it would be if we were favored with large endowments; yet, what will be secured as the reward of persevering effort will be the more valuable trophy.

In our faithful onward course we know we shall have the best wishes of this community. May we enjoy the smiles of a benignant Providence.

Professors and Instructors in the University of the City of New York.

ISAAC FERRIS, D.D., LL.D., CHANCELLOR.

I. Preparatory Department.

PRINCIPALS.

DAVID BENDAN, Ph. D., Classical Department and German.
THEODORE COLEMAN, A.M., English and Mathematical Department.

ASSOCIATE PRINCIPAL.

MOSES M. HOBBY, Primary Department.

A. WOLF, M.D., Professor of French and Spanish.
J. B. BROWN, Professor of Elocution.
MARTIN S. PAINE, Instructor in Book-Keeping.
DAVID STANTON, Instructor in Penmanship.
B. H. COE, Instructor in Drawing and Painting.

II. Collegiate Department.

REV. ISAAC FERRIS, D.D, LL.D.,

Professor of Moral Philosophy and the Evidences of Revealed Religion.

E. A. JOHNSON, A.M.,

Professor of the Latin Language and Literature.

JOHN W. DRAPER, M.D., LL.D.,

Professor of Chemistry and Natural History.

ELIAS LOOMIS, LL.D.,

Professor of Mathematics, Natural Philosophy and Astronomy.

HOWARD CROSBY, A.M.,

Professor of the Greek Language and Literature.

REV. BENJAMIN N. MARTIN, A.M.,

Professor of Intellectual Philosophy, History and Belles-Lettres.

RICHARD H. BULL, A.M.,

Professor of Civil Engineering.

THEO. D'OREMIEULX,
Professor of the French Language and Literature.

Professor of the Spanish Language.

VINCENZO BOTTA, Ph. D.,
Professor of the Italian Language and Literature.

DAVID BENDAN, Ph. D.,
Professor of the German Language and Literature.

Rev. PAUL C. SINDING,
Professor of the Scandinavian Language and Literature.

III. Professional Schools.

SCHOOL OF ART.

S. F. B. Morse, LL.D., Professor of Literature of Arts, of Design.

Thomas S. Cummings, N.A., Professor of Arts of Design.

SCHOOL OF CIVIL ENGINEERING.

Richard H. Bull, A.M., Professor of Civil Engineering.

Thomas S. Cummings. N.A., Professor of Architectural Drawing.

SCHOOL OF ANALYTICAL AND PRACTICAL CHEMISTRY.

John W. Draper, M.D., LL.D., Professor of Chemistry.

John C. Draper, M.D., Professor of Analytical and Practical Chemistry.

SCHOOL OF MEDICINE.

Valentine Mott, M.D., LL.D., Emeritus Professor of Surgery and Surgical Anatomy, and Ex-President of the Faculty.

Martyn Paine, M.D., LL.D., Professor of Materia Medica and Therapeutics.

Gunning S. Bedford, M.D., Professor of Obstetrics, the Diseases of Women and Children, and Clinical Midwifery.

John W. Draper, M.D., LL.D., Professor of Chemistry and Physiology.

Alfred C. Post, M.D., Professor of the Principles and Operations of Surgery, with Surgical and Pathological Anatomy.

WILLIAM H. VAN BUREN, M.D., Professor of General and Descriptive Anatomy.

JOHN T. METCALFE, M.D., Professor of the Institutes and Practice of Medicine.

T. C. FINNELL, M.D., Demonstrator of Anatomy.

ALEXANDER B. MOTT, M.D., Prosector to the Emeritus Professor of Surgery.

J. HINTON, M.D., Prosector to the Professor of Surgery.

SUMMER COURSE.

T. C. FINNELL, M.D., on Pathological Anatomy.

T. GAILLARD THOMAS, M.D., on Obstetrical Operations.

P. A. AYLETT, M.D, on Physiology.

WILLIAM R. DONAGHE, M.D., on Surgical Anatomy.

GODFREY AIGNER, M.D., on Medical Botany.

CYRUS RAMSAY, M.D., on Medical Jurisprudence.

School of Law.

HON. THOMAS W. CLERKE,

Justice of the Supreme Court of the State of New York, Professor of the General Theory and Practice of American Law, including Municipal Law and Equity Jurisprudence.

Professor of International, Constitutional and Statutory Law, and Law of Damages.

HON. LEVI S. CHATFIELD,

Late Attorney General of the State of New York, Professor of Criminal Law and Medical Jurisprudence.

PETER Y. CUTLER, ESQ.,

Counsellor at Law, Professor of Civil Law, the Law of Evidence, Pleading, and Practice, and the Law of Real Property.

WILLIAM B. WEDGWOOD, A.M.,

Counsellor at Law, Professor of Commercial, Maritime, and Parliamentary Law, and Law of Personal Property.

GEORGE H. MOORE, A.M., ESQ.,

Professor of Legal History and Literature.

𝔖𝔠𝔥𝔢𝔪𝔢 𝔬𝔣 𝔇𝔞𝔦𝔩𝔶 𝔖𝔱𝔲𝔡𝔦𝔢𝔰

OF

THE COLLEGIATE COURSE.

HOURS.	FIRST TERM.	HOURS.	SECOND TERM.	HOURS.	THIRD TERM.
FRESHMEN YEAR.					
1	Mathematics.	1	†Greek.	1	Greek.
2	†Greek.	2	Mathematics.	2	Latin.
3	Latin.	3	Rhetoric.	3	Mathematics.
SOPHOMORE *YEAR.					
1	Modern History.	1	Mathematics.	1	Mathematics.
2	Mathematics.	2	English Literature.	2	Political Economy.
3	†Greek.	3	Latin.	3	Latin.
JUNIOR †YEAR.					
1	Greek.	1	Logic.	1	Natural Theology.
2	Intellectual Philosophy.	2	Latin.	2	Greek.
3	Mechanics, Hydrostatics.	3	Pneumatics, Acoustics, Optics.	3	Astronomy.
SENIOR †YEAR.					
1	Moral Science and Constitutional Law.	1	Evidences of Rev. Religion.	1	Latin.
2	Latin.	2	Greek.	2	International Law.
3	Chemistry.	3	Chemistry.	3	Geology.

** Modern Languages, when desired, are pursued in a fourth hour, viz :
French—Tuesday and Thursday, at 1, P. M.
German—Wednesday and Friday, at 1, P. M.

* Compositions and Declamations in the class on alternate Mondays.

† Essays and Reviews alternately at intervals. Forensic Discussions on the last Monday of each month.

During the Freshmen and Sophomore years, the Greek Professor lectures each Monday on Greek History; during the Junior year, on Greek Literature; and in the Senior year. on Greek Philosophy.

The University has always allowed students, with consent of their parents, to take a course in Mathematical and English studies, without the Classics. The Faculty of Science and Letters feeling the importance of making such course as complete as possible, have recently adopted the following, which they commend to the attention of parents.

Scheme of Daily Studies

OF

THE SCIENTIFIC COURSE.

	HOURS	FIRST TERM.	HOURS	SECOND TERM.	HOURS	THIRD TERM.
First Year.	1	Algebra.	1	Christian Evidences.	1	Botany.
	2	Natural Science.	2	Algebra.	2	German.
	3	German.	3	Rhetoric.	3	Geometry.
Second Year.	1	Modern History.	1	Surveying and Navigation.	1	Analytic Geometry, Calculus.
	2	Geometry and Trigonometry.	2	English Literature.	2	Political Economy.
	3	Chemistry.	3	Chemistry.	3	Geology.
Third Year.	1	Moral Science and Constitutional Law.	1	Logic.	1	Natural Theology.
	2	Intellectual Philosophy.	2	Physiology.	2	International Law.
	3	Mechanics and Hydrostatics.	3	Philosophy, Pneumatics, Acoustics, Optics.	3	Astronomy.

The exercises in Composition and Declamation are the same as in the Collegiate course.

Students who complete this course, together with Civil Engineering, and pass satisfactory examinations, will receive the degree of Bachelor of Science.